The Wish Master

THE
WISH
MASTER

Betty Ren Wright

SCHOLASTIC INC.

New York Toronto London Auckland Sydney
Mexico City New Delhi Hong Kong Buenos Aires

ISBN 0-439-42977-3

12 11 10 9 8 7 6 5 4 3   2 3 4 5 6 7/0

Printed in the U.S.A.   40

First Scholastic printing, June 2002

For Jean and Cliff Gehrt, dear friends always,
and my neighbors in spirit
wherever they live

Contents

CHAPTER ONE
"If You're Not Too Chicken!"

"That's one broken-down old boat," Corby said. He hoped Buck Miller wasn't going to want to go for a ride. "Anybody can tell that boat would sink like a rock."

"It would not," Buck retorted. "Where'd you learn so much about boats?"

Corby said, "At camp," and then wished he hadn't. He'd met Buck less than an hour ago, and already they were talking about things Corby didn't want to talk about. Or even think about.

"My dad knows everything there is to know about boats," he added quickly. "He goes sailing with his boss. On the ocean!"

Buck hopped off the little pier into the rowboat and stood with his feet wide apart, rocking from side to side, showing off. "So where's your dad now?" he demanded.

"Home," Corby said. "In Santa Barbara. He couldn't come here with my mom and me because he has to work."

Buck rocked the boat harder. Then he pointed across the river. "See that farmhouse over there? That's the Millikens' place, and they've got five Lab puppies. We can row over there and see them if you're not too chicken."

"I'm not!" Corby snapped. Why had Buck said that? He wondered if being scared of stuff stuck out for everyone to see, like freckles or big ears.

"Well, I'm going," Buck said. "And you'd better not tell anyone. Got that?"

Corby got it. He understood that Buck wasn't supposed to row across the river. The boat was probably just as rickety as it looked.

"You can pick wildflowers for your mama, little boy," Buck added, waving an arm at the field behind them. "Unless you're afraid of bumblebees."

Corby crouched at the edge of the pier, his heart thumping. He wanted to see the puppies, maybe even persuade his mom to buy him one. Mostly, though, he wanted to show Buck that he wasn't afraid. If they were going to be friends while Corby was in Wisconsin, it had to start now. He stepped down into the boat.

Buck loosened the rope that held them to the pier and dipped the oars into the water. "They're really neat puppies," he said, sounding more friendly. "I know because we got one of our dogs from the last litter."

The space between the boat and the pier began to grow. Corby was glad he knew how to swim. He wasn't fast, but it had been one thing he'd done as well as most of the other boys at Camp Macaho.

He wished he could forget he'd ever gone to camp. Until this summer it hadn't mattered much that he was the smallest, skinniest kid in his class. He and his two best friends knew more about computers than anyone else—even more than their teachers. The three of them collected baseball cards and insects and miniature cars, and everything had been great until his mother heard about Camp Macaho at a PTA meeting.

"I'm sure you'll enjoy it," she'd said. "You have to try new things if you want to be well-rounded, Corby. Think about all the fun things your father did at camp when he was a boy in Wisconsin."

Corby didn't care a hoot about being well-rounded. But when his dad said, "Camp is probably a good idea," and "Just be a good sport, Corb," he knew he was on his way.

Things had started going wrong the very first day at Macaho. There was that rocky cliff behind the mess hall, Corby remembered. His dad might have thought climbing the cliff would be fun, but Corby couldn't make himself try it, even when the other kids scrambled over it like monkeys. Why take a chance? One slip and you could get yourself killed.

He'd hated horseback riding, too. Any horse, even the oldest and laziest, felt as big as an elephant when you were on top of it. And he still had nightmares about that so-called bridge over Macaho Creek. It was nothing but a single plank that quivered and bucked when the boys ran across it. Corby had gotten halfway across just once, and then his legs wouldn't take him any farther. He'd had to back up on his hands and knees till he reached the shore.

Camp Macaho had been the worst thing—the only really bad thing—that had ever happened to him.

"I'm going to camp next summer," Buck said suddenly. "Which one did you go to?"

"It's in California," Corby said. "There's lots of just as good ones here in Wisconsin." He didn't want Buck to go where anyone would remember Corby Hill.

The boat was in the middle of the river now, jerking from side to side because Buck wasn't a good rower. Corby sat still, with his arms wrapped around his knees, and wondered if the last part of this summer was going to be any better than the first part. He'd hardly had time to unpack his suitcase and turn on his computer before Grandpa Hill had called from Berry Hill to say he needed help taking care of Grandma. She'd had a heart attack and needed lots of rest.

His mom had started planning right away. "Your father will feel better knowing we're taking care of his folks," she said firmly, when Corby looked glum. "By the time school starts, I'm sure Grandpa and Grandma will be able to manage on their own again."

A harsh, grating noise interrupted Corby's thoughts. Buck whooped and dug an oar so deeply into the water that the boat swung around.

"What're you doing?" Corby yelled. He saw water in the bottom of the boat.

The grating sound came again, followed by an ugly *crrrunch*. "What do you think I'm doing?" Buck panted. "I'm trying to move us. We've hit a rock or something!"

Corby stared at the crack opening up at his feet. "How deep is the water here?" he asked hoarsely.

"How do I know?" Buck said. "I can't swim." There was a quiver in his voice.

The crunching and scraping went on. "If there's rocks, maybe it's shallow here," Corby said. "Stop rowing. I'll see if I can stand up."

He stepped over the side while Buck leaned the other way to keep the boat from tipping. To Corby's relief, his toes touched rock right away— smooth, slippery, and solid. It was going to be all right! Then he took a step toward shore and the rock ended. Before he could take a breath, he'd plunged straight to the bottom.

CHAPTER TWO
"You Saved My Life!"

When Corby came up sputtering, Buck was still sitting in the boat, but the water was up to his middle. The sides of the boat were just a couple of inches above the water, so he looked as if he were in a wide wooden bathtub.

"Do you know how to float?" Corby asked, his teeth chattering.

Buck stared at him and clung to the sides of the boat.

"Listen, you hang on one end of an oar and kick with your feet," Corby said. "I'll hold on to the other end and swim, okay?"

He grabbed an oar and pushed the paddle end toward Buck, just as the boat slurped and slithered beneath the surface. Then he started to swim, towing the oar behind him.

It was hard work. He splashed a lot and gulped big mouthfuls of the river. After a few strokes, he let one foot drop, feeling for the bottom. Nothing!

He swam a few more feet and tried again. This time his toes touched the bottom. It was muddy and unpleasant, but it was there. He started walking to the shore, with Buck clinging to the paddle and splashing noisily behind him.

When they were back on the riverbank at last, they pulled off their shirts and sat shivering in the sun. Corby looked for the spot where they had gotten snagged on the rock. There was no sign of the boat. The second oar drifted slowly down the river.

"Hey, man, you saved my life," Buck said, when he'd caught his breath. "That was really cool! You're a great swimmer."

Corby realized that Buck didn't know he had walked most of the way to the shore. "You'd have been okay," he said modestly. "We could have waited there on the rock till somebody saw us, I guess."

But Buck shook his head. "No way! We don't want anybody to know we were out there. My dad would blow his top."

"Was it his boat?" Corby asked.

"It was nobody's boat," Buck said. "Just a junker. But we can't tell, just the same. I'm supposed to stay away from the river till I learn how to swim. If my dad finds out, I'll be grounded for the rest of the summer."

Corby sighed. He would have liked his family to hear he'd saved his new friend's life, but he knew Buck was right. His own mother would be frightened and angry if she heard what happened. Even worse, Grandpa Hill would probably say something like, "Your father would never have gotten into a leaky old tub like that." Or, "Your father swam across the river every day when he was your age. It's no big deal." If he didn't say it, he'd think it, which would be almost as bad.

"Listen," Buck said, "I bet you learned a lot of other stuff besides swimming at camp, right?"

"Like what?" Corby asked cautiously.

"Did you go on hikes?"

"Sure."

"At night?"

"Once." Now what? Corby wondered. Buck Miller was turning out to be a bundle of bad ideas!

"The reason I'm asking," Buck explained, "is because there's a place I want to go to, but it has to be at night—at midnight. Otherwise it won't work."

"What won't work?" Corby asked.

Buck rolled his eyes. "Just wait! The guys in my class are all too chicken to go at night, and that's why I'm asking you. You're no chicken."

Corby blinked. He was glad Buck had changed his mind, but he could see how that might be dangerous, too. Being brave Buck-style would mean taking chances.

"Well, I can't go," Corby told him. "My mom would never let me."

Buck stood up. "She won't know, city boy," he said briskly, as if it were all settled. "You can sneak out, same as me." He flapped his shirt to help it dry and pulled his damp shorts away from his seat. "I'll be outside your grandpa's place at eleven o'clock tonight," he said. "So don't fall asleep. This'll be the biggest thing that ever happened to you!"

CHAPTER THREE
The Wish Master

"I'm glad Buck Miller stopped by," Grandma Hill said at supper that night. It was the first time she'd eaten with them since they arrived. "You two can have fun together this summer." She patted Corby's hand with her too-thin freckled one.

Grandpa Hill grunted. He was a giant of a man who had been a farmer most of his life. The skin around his eyes looked old, but his eyes didn't. They said all kinds of things, like *What would this runt know about having fun?*

Corby had overheard Grandpa call him that the first night they were in Berry Hill: *the runt of the litter*. Grandpa and Grandma had seven other grandchildren who lived in New York and Florida. Corby hadn't seen them for a long time, but he'd seen pictures. The boys were all big and broad shouldered. They looked the way Corby's own dad must have looked when he was a kid. The girls were tall, too.

"Buck's all right," Grandpa said in his gruff voice. "Strong as an ox and a hard worker. He'll be a big help on their farm when he grows up."

Corby sighed and pushed back his chair. "Is it okay if I watch television?"

His mother nodded, and Corby escaped to the living room, but not before Grandma made him feel even worse.

"Being big isn't everything," she said loudly, so he would be sure to hear. She felt sorry for him.

He wished he could tell his grandparents that he had saved strong-as-an-ox Buck's life this very afternoon. What would they say if they knew tonight he was going to a secret place where Buck's other friends were afraid to go?

If I decide to do it, he added, but he knew that he would. Buck had said, "You're no chicken." Corby whispered the words to himself a couple of times. True or not, they sounded good.

* * *

12

The house was quiet when Corby started down the stairs at ten minutes to eleven. The first step creaked loudly, and so did the second. He held his breath. The house seemed different in the dark.

Cautiously, he swung one leg over the banister, clinging to the rail with both hands so he wouldn't shoot down like a rocket. At the bottom he slid off and tiptoed to the front door.

The key hung from the little knob at the top of the hinge. Corby felt like a burglar as he found the keyhole with his fingers and slipped the key into place. He could imagine Grandpa charging out of the back bedroom with his rifle in his hands.

Out on the porch, he stopped for a moment to get used to the dark. Then he edged along the front of the house to the long row of lilac bushes. It was even darker there.

"Hurry up, will you?" The whispery growl made Corby jump. He squinted and saw Buck crouched under the lilacs, close to the road.

"Hurry up!" Buck growled again. "We have a long way to go. The road is the easiest part."

The gravel road was pale gray in the moonlight. Corby stepped into a rut and fell flat. "You call this easy?" he muttered. He wiggled his ankle, hoping for a sprain.

Buck didn't even look back. "I've got a flash-light," he said. "Can't use it here. Somebody might see us."

They passed three small summer cottages, all as dark and silent as Grandpa's house, and then the road cut through meadows of tall grass. Corby blinked when Buck suddenly turned right.

"Hey!" he exclaimed. "Where—"

"There's a path," Buck said. "It's sort of narrow."

Corby couldn't see any path at all. He plunged into the grass, keeping his eyes on Buck and wish-ing he were home in bed. Home in Santa Barbara, he thought. A million miles away from Buck Miller and his dumb ideas.

The meadow seemed to go on forever. When Corby looked over his shoulder, he couldn't see the road. He hoped Buck knew where they were going. Otherwise they could tramp around like this all night.

"Okay," Buck said unexpectedly. "Now we can use the flashlight." A thin beam cut through the darkness. It lit what looked like a solid wall of trees and underbrush right ahead of them.

"No way!" Corby exclaimed before he could stop himself. "I'm not going in there!"

"We have to," Buck said. He swung the flashlight from side to side. "Look for three big sticks leaning against one another like a tepee. That's where the path begins."

"How do you know?" Corby demanded.

"Because I put them there," Buck said. "In the daytime. It's easy to find the path in the daytime." He moved slowly along the line of trees until he found the marker. "Gotcha!" he exclaimed happily. "Come on!"

Corby peered over Buck's shoulder. "That isn't a real path," he complained. "You're going to get us lost for sure!"

"Won't," Buck retorted. He ducked under a low branch, and Corby had to move fast before the flashlight beam disappeared. There was nothing else to do but follow it.

The woods were hot. Mosquitoes danced around Corby's ears. For a few minutes they pushed ahead without speaking, ducking under branches, climbing over a huge log, and bumping into each other.

"It's uphill from here on," Buck said, puffing a little. "Stay on the path, because we'll get pretty close to the edge."

Corby smacked a mosquito on his forehead. "The edge of what?"

"The cliff!" Buck said impatiently. "The river's right over there." He swung his arm to the right and started climbing again.

The path got worse at every step. Tree roots stretched like snakes in the bobbing beam of the flashlight. A loud rustling brought both boys to a stop.

"Hope that wasn't a bear," Buck said. "What did you do about bears when you hiked at camp?"

"Nothing," Corby said. The only night "hike" he'd gone on at Camp Macaho was when the boys in his cabin had decided they wanted sodas from the machine on the porch of the lodge. Sneaking across the camp's smooth lawn had been nothing like this.

"Listen," Buck said, seeming to forget about the bear. "You can hear the river. That means we're nearly to the top of the cliff. It sort of hangs out over the water."

The beam of light started moving again, and the path grew steeper. Corby stumbled over a root. When he looked up, he saw Buck clearly for the first time since they'd entered the woods. He had reached an open place at the end of the path.

"We made it!" Buck exclaimed.

Corby stepped out onto a rocky floor. The air was cool and sweet, but the rushing water sounded very close.

"Where's the river?" he asked nervously.

Buck pointed with the flashlight. They were standing a foot or so from the edge of the cliff. Then he swung the light sharply to the left, and when it stopped, what Corby saw nearly made him jump out of his sneakers.

A huge figure towered over them, blocking out the stars. Its body was a rough column of rock covered with strange markings; its head was a mammoth skull-shaped boulder. Corby shuddered as the light settled on the monster's face. He—it—was smiling hideously.

"How about that?" Buck demanded. He sounded proud but a little scared, too. "That's the Wish Master. He's been here about a thousand years, and he can do anything. If you make a wish at exactly midnight, it'll come true every time!"

Corby wanted to say Buck was crazy, but he couldn't. All he could do was stare. The monster stared back, its smile seeming to grow wider and nastier every second.

"Okay, get ready!" Buck ordered. "It's almost—"

A shrill clang interrupted him. Corby yelped in terror and jumped backward. He teetered on the edge of the cliff.

"Midnight!" Buck exclaimed. "I brought my alarm clock so we wouldn't miss it." He faced the stone monster and started talking fast.

"I wish for a mountain bike. Silver and blue." He paused. "Your turn, city boy."

His head spinning, Corby said the first thing he thought of. "VAROOM!" VAROOM! was the name of a video game he'd wanted for months. Then he turned his back on the monster. "Let's go," he said.

"Right," Buck agreed cheerfully. He ducked around Corby and started back down the path. "All we have to do now is go home and wait."

CHAPTER FOUR
The Second Wish

Corby had reached the top of the stairs when he heard footsteps coming down the hall. Grandpa was up. He sank back against the wall and held his breath until the steps stopped and the bathroom light clicked on. Then he scooted into his bedroom.

It had been a narrow escape. Quickly, he kicked off his sneakers and slid under the covers. He pulled the sheet up to his chin to hide his clothes, but even then he didn't feel safe. Grandpa's sharp gaze could probably see through anything.

When he opened his eyes again, the bedroom was full of sunshine. Downstairs, the doorbell was ringing. He jumped out of bed, changed into clean jeans and his Santa Barbara T-shirt, and hurried to the bathroom to splash cold water on his face.

At the foot of the stairs he stopped for a minute to listen to Grandpa's deep voice and his mother's gentle one in the kitchen.

"—I locked that door last night, same as always," Grandpa said. "Are you sure you didn't go out early this morning?"

"I'm sure," Corby's mother said. "Maybe you forgot this one time. You have a lot on your mind."

"I didn't forget."

Corby groaned. Forget breakfast! he thought, even though his stomach was growling. He couldn't lie to Grandpa about the door, but telling the truth was impossible, too.

He was about to sneak back upstairs when he saw a package lying on the hall table. It was addressed in big black letters: CORBY HILL.

His mother came out of the kitchen. "I was just going to call you, sleepyhead," she said. "Guess what—a present came for you a few minutes ago. Why don't you open it while I take Grandma's breakfast upstairs?"

Corby stopped worrying about Grandpa and the unlocked door. His heart gave a little lurch as he picked up the package. It was the size of a video game. He tore off the brown paper. It *was* a video game—not VAROOM!, but another racing game that looked as if it might be pretty good. And that meant—he could hardly believe it—that meant the Wish Master was real!

"What did Dad send you?" his mother asked as she came back down the stairs. "You look about to pop!"

Corby showed her the game. Then he picked up the wrapping paper. Sure enough, their home address in Santa Barbara was printed in the left-hand corner. And the package had been mailed a couple of days ago, long before he'd made his wish. Still . . .

"Why so serious?" His mother patted his shoulder. "Dad said he was afraid you wouldn't have enough to do here, so he decided to surprise you. Want to call him this evening and say thanks?"

"Sure." Corby started toward the den and the television set, then changed his mind. There was something else he had to do before he tried the new game.

Fifteen minutes dragged by before he could call Buck. With Grandpa out in the garden and his mother back upstairs taking care of Grandma, he finally had the kitchen to himself.

"It worked!" he exclaimed into the phone as soon as Buck said hello. "I got a video game in the mail this morning!"

Buck whistled. "Are you kidding? You really got it?"

"Not the one I asked for," Corby admitted. "But it's sort of like it. Did you get the bike?"

"Not yet," Buck said, but he sounded hopeful. "Maybe it'll still happen. Or maybe—maybe I didn't ask the right way. How did you say it?"

Corby tried to remember the exact words he'd used. He was usually polite when he was asking for something, but last night had been different. He'd been too scared to think. "Don't remember," he said at last.

"Well, I'm going to try again," Buck said excitedly. "Let's go back tonight—if I don't get the bike today, that is."

"I can't—" Corby began, but that was as far as he got.

"Somebody's coming," Buck interrupted. "See you at eleven." The receiver clicked at the other end of the line.

Corby picked up the video game and headed toward the den. He didn't want to take another long hike in the dark, but Buck hadn't given him a chance to say no. And maybe it wasn't such a bad idea after all. He would have a chance to make a different wish. Now that he knew the Wish Master really did have magic powers, he would wish for something bigger than a video game. He would ask for a dog.

He'd been playing the new game for just a few minutes when he realized Grandpa was watching him from the doorway.

"I can't see any sense to that business," he said. "Just a lot of racket. Probably disturbing your grandma, too."

Corby turned down the sound. "It's a race," he explained. "You pick a car and try—"

"Never mind," Grandpa said gruffly. "I'm not interested. You shouldn't be hunched in front of the tube when you could be outside getting some exercise. Or even doing a little work. I'm going to replace a few stones in the front walk, and I could use some help."

"Okay." Corby switched off the VCR and followed Grandpa through the house, out the back door, and across the lawn to the toolshed. He felt the same way he felt at school before a big test.

Grandpa lifted one shovel, then another, and handed the lighter one to Corby. "Your pa and I put in this walk when he was only a year or so older than you," he said as they marched around the side of the house to the front yard. "He worked harder than I did—wanted to surprise his ma when she came home from town."

Corby stared at the curving path of stepping-stones, lined on either side with rosebushes. The stones looked as if they'd been there forever.

"You start digging around that one." Grandpa pointed to a stone that had a deep crack across the middle. "I'll get a new one from behind the shed."

Corby waited until Grandpa disappeared around the side of the house. Then he lifted the shovel and jabbed downward with all his strength. The blade skittered across the hard ground and struck the stone. He tried again with the same result. The third time, the earth crumbled a little. By then, drops of sweat were running down his face and he was panting. At this rate it was going to take all day to dig up one stone.

Dozens of tiny ants began running across the stone in all directions. Corby crouched to watch and catch his breath. He liked ants. They were small, but you could see they believed whatever they were doing was really important. His pounding shovel must have seemed like an earthquake to them. Right now they were probably yelling to one another to run away before the earthquake started again.

"I'm glad I'm not paying you by the hour!"

Corby rocked back on his heels. Grandpa had come around the corner of the house with a stepping-stone under one arm. He looked down at the narrow groove Corby had managed to dig on one side of the stone.

"The ground's really hard," Corby mumbled. He wished he hadn't stopped to look at the ants.

Grandpa laid the stone in the grass and picked up a shovel. "Needs some muscle, that's all," he said without looking at Corby. "Nothing gets done if you give up."

Corby's face burned. He watched the shovel move up and down, sinking deeper into the earth with every stroke.

"Go get the wheelbarrow," Grandpa ordered. "Back of the toolshed."

Corby was glad to escape. He found the wheelbarrow, next to a whole pile of new stepping-stones, and pushed it around to the front of the house just as Grandpa pried the cracked stone loose and lifted it out of its bed. Then he slid the new stone into place and began smoothing the earth around it.

"Where do you want the old stone to go?" Corby asked timidly. "I can move it."

Grandpa grunted. "Can you?" he asked. He stood up and watched Corby struggle to lift the stone. It was too heavy. He could tip it on edge, but he couldn't get it off the ground. When he'd tried three or four times, Grandpa picked up the stone and dropped it into the wheelbarrow with a thump.

"You push this around to the back and dump the rock under the kitchen windows," he said. "I might put a rock garden in there, if your grandma wants it. After that you can—do whatever you want. This is no job for you."

"Fine," Corby said. It was his "who cares?" voice, the one he used when he didn't get picked for a team at school. Grandpa looked up at him sharply and then went back to his digging. "But if you're going to sit in front of the tube all morning, you keep the sound down low," he ordered. "Way low."

Corby pushed the wheelbarrow around the house and dumped the rock under the kitchen windows. It broke into two pieces when it landed. He stomped one of them, then the other, hoping to break them again, but they didn't crack. Then he pushed the wheelbarrow back behind the toolshed, ramming it hard against the pile of new stones.

He hated stupid stone walks. He hated Berry Hill. It wasn't even a town, just a jumble of farms and summer cottages, with a couple of stores and a church at a crossroads. And he especially hated people who expected him to do things he couldn't possibly do.

It's a good thing we're going back to the Wish Master tonight, he thought furiously. It's a really good thing. Because now he had something important to wish for, and it wasn't a dog. Oh, he still wanted the dog, but there was something else he wanted more.

He wanted to go home tomorrow. Day after tomorrow, at the latest. Not at the end of the summer.

CHAPTER FIVE
"I'll Never Get My Bike!"

"It's a good thing you came to Berry Hill this summer," Buck said. "Otherwise I still wouldn't know for sure how great the Wish Master is." He'd been talking, in a loud whisper, almost every step of the way down the dark road and across the meadow. When he wasn't talking, he whistled softly through his teeth.

"I thought you did know," Corby whispered back. "You said all we had to do was make a wish at midnight, remember?"

"Right," Buck agreed cheerfully. "And it turned out to be true! What are you going to wish for this time? You ought to ask for something bigger than a video game."

Corby hesitated. Buck had just said he was glad Corby had come to Wisconsin. It would be sort of mean to say, *I'm going to wish I can go home tomorrow.*

"I was going to ask for a dog," he said finally. "But I'm still thinking."

He had brought his own flashlight this time, borrowed from a kitchen drawer earlier in the day. The extra light made this hike a little less scary. Even so, he shivered when they reached the edge of the woods. Just about anything might be waiting in there. A bear could walk right up behind them, and they wouldn't know it until it was too late.

"All *right!*" Buck pointed his flashlight at the three sticks that marked the beginning of the path. "Here we go!"

Together they stepped into the deeper darkness under the trees.

"I'm getting really good at this!" Buck exclaimed. He sounded so pleased with himself, and so glad to be where they were, that Corby wanted to punch him. Didn't he know how dangerous this was?

Buck moved quickly, and they soon began to climb. "Watch your step," he called over his shoulder. "It's a long way down to the water."

"Big joke!" Corby muttered. Sweat soaked his T-shirt, and he itched. Mosquitoes tickled his ears. He had to keep reminding himself this would all be worth it, if the Wish Master helped him go home.

"Okay, we made it!" Buck laughed out loud as he pushed aside some branches and stepped out into the clearing that marked the top of the cliff. "Come on! It's nearly time."

Stars glittered overhead, and the air up here was cool. Corby swung his flashlight toward the back of the clearing.

The Wish Master was even bigger than Corby remembered. Uglier, too. His smile was mean, as if he knew how scary he was and liked it that way.

"Did you bring the alarm clock?" Corby whispered.

Buck reached into the pocket of his shorts and shone his flashlight on the face of the little clock.

"Two minutes," he said hoarsely.

They moved closer to the Wish Master and waited. Corby wasn't sure whether the sound he heard was the ticking of the clock or the pounding of his own heart. Even though he was expecting it, the squawk of the alarm made him jump.

"Please, I'd like a mountain bike," Buck said loudly, almost stuttering in his eagerness. "If it isn't too much trouble. Thank you very much."

He stepped back and Corby took his place. "I'd like a dog," he said. Then he lowered his voice and spoke very fast. "And I want to go home. I don't want to stay at my grandpa's house all summer. *Please!*"

"What did you say?" Buck demanded. "After you asked for the dog?"

Corby didn't answer. He swung his flashlight around till he found the path.

Buck pushed past him. "If you wished for two things, that's not fair," he said angrily. "Maybe you made the Wish Master mad, being greedy like that. I'll never get my bike!"

"I'm not greedy," Corby said. But Buck's anger had taken him by surprise. Silently, they made their way down the hill, moving so fast that there was no time to worry about what might be lurking in the dark.

When they reached the meadow, Buck whirled around and leveled his flashlight beam at Corby's face.

"You tell me what you wished for up there," he ordered. "I need to know."

31

Corby ducked away from the light and kept walking. What was the use of talking? He hoped Buck would get a bike. He hoped he would get a dog himself. But most of all he hoped he'd soon be on his way home to Santa Barbara. Maybe it wasn't fair, but he was glad he'd made that second wish.

The next few days were long ones. Each time the phone rang, Corby expected it to be his dad. *I'm lonesome,* he might say. *Come on home, Corby.* Usually, though, the caller was an old friend who wanted to know how Grandma Hill was feeling. Grandpa's voice was heavy as he answered their questions.

"Poor man, he's so sad," Corby's mother murmured. "He used to enjoy talking with neighbors, but not anymore. I think Grandma's illness has changed him more than it has her."

Corby couldn't remember Grandpa any other way than he was now. "Why does he have to be so crabby all the time?" he muttered. "He doesn't like anybody—especially me."

His mother looked shocked. "Of course he likes you, Corby!" she exclaimed. "He loves you! He's just very worried right now. And besides that, he hasn't seen you since you were in kindergarten—give him time to get to know you again."

Corby knew she wanted to make him feel better. Still, she must have noticed how Grandpa was always finding fault with him. *Turn down that television—you'll disturb your grandma. . . . Stop running up and down the stairs like a herd of elephants. . . . Go outside and do something. . . .*

He didn't want Corby around. Anyone could see that.

"Call Buck and see if he'd like to go for a hike," his mother suggested. "That would be fun."

"Maybe," Corby said. But he knew he wouldn't do it. Grandpa didn't like him, and Buck didn't either. If only the Wish Master would work his magic, he could forget them both.

CHAPTER SIX
"The Ugliest Animal
I've Ever Seen!"

Corby crouched at the end of the pier and stared across the river. The field on the other side was lined with row after perfect row of cabbages. Beyond the field stood a barn, and beyond that was the gray farmhouse where a family of Labrador puppies were waiting for someone who needed a dog. At least, that's what Buck had said. He wondered if Buck had made that up to get Corby into the leaky old boat.

Four days had passed since the second visit to the Wish Master. Neither of Corby's wishes had come true, and with each passing hour, he was more sure they never would. Something had gone wrong. Maybe Buck was right; maybe the Wish Master didn't like people who asked for too much.

Most of the time Corby had stayed in his
bedroom, reading, but once in a while he came
out here to skip stones and splash around close
to shore. He'd had to promise his mom he
wouldn't swim by himself, but she hadn't men-
tioned wading. Anything was better than watching Grandpa tramp back and forth, pushing
wheelbarrow loads of dirt and stones for the new
rock garden.

"Working on the rock garden helps him feel
close to Grandma," Corby's mother said, "even
when she's too tired or weak to talk with him. It's
going to be his surprise for her when she's well
enough to go outside again."

Today Grandpa had carried the invalid
downstairs for lunch. He moved slowly, his face
red with effort, and Corby's mother walked in
front of them. When Grandma saw Corby, she
smiled.

"It's too bad you couldn't bring your computer
with you, Corby," she said. "Your mother says
you're a real expert on that machine. If you had it
with you, you could give Grandpa and me some
lessons. Wouldn't that be nice, Henry?"

Grandpa grunted. The grunt could have
meant yes or no.

"Some farmers use computers," Corby's mother said. "I read an article about it. The computer tells them what to plant and where."

Grandpa grunted again, a definite *no* this time. "Never needed a machine to tell *me* what to do," he grumbled.

Remembering, Corby threw a stone with extra force. It skipped five times before it sank.

"Not bad!"

The voice was right behind him. He turned and saw Buck searching for a flat stone to throw. Buck's shorts and shirt were streaked with dirt. Gray dust coated his bare arms and legs, and there was a smudge on his nose.

"I've been cleaning out our old barn," he said. "It's a real mess."

"Looks like it," Corby said. He wondered why Buck had come back. Was he going to ask Corby to help him clean the barn?

"Guess what just happened!" Buck grinned unexpectedly, and Corby felt a tingle of excitement. "My dad just said I'm doing a great job, and if I work this hard the rest of the week, I can order the mountain bike I want from the catalog!"

"Wow!" Corby stared at him. "That's great!"

It was better than great. Another wish had come true, and this time it was a big one. The Wish Master really could do whatever you asked.

"So now you can get your dog," Buck said generously. "It's okay with me." Then he scowled. "Or do you already have it?"

"No way." But Corby was suddenly dizzy with hope. Maybe his dad would call tonight to say he should fly home right away. Maybe he'd say, "I've got a surprise here waiting for you," and the surprise would turn out to be a puppy. It was possible.

"I don't even care if you did make two wishes," Buck went on. "Just so I get my bike!" He scooped up a handful of pebbles and threw them as far as he could. Corby did the same thing, and soon they were having a contest to see who could throw the farthest and yell the loudest.

When they got tired of throwing, they sat close to the river's edge and wiggled their bare toes in the water.

"You can use my old bike as soon as I get the new one," Buck offered. "There's a raspberry patch about two miles from here. I'll show you."

"Sounds neat," Corby said carefully. He would be back in Santa Barbara before the new bike arrived.

"You have to watch out for bears, though," Buck said. "They like raspberries."

A cloud drifted across the sun, making the water feel chilly. Corby put on his sneakers. "I'd better go," he said. "My grandpa will be mad if I'm late for supper."

They saw the dog as soon as they stood up. It was about twenty feet away, partly hidden by meadow grass. One dark eye and one pale ice-blue eye watched them from behind a fringe of straggly gray hair.

Buck snickered. "Now, there's the ugliest animal I've ever seen!" he exclaimed. "Did you ever see a dog as ugly as that in California?"

"Let's just go," Corby said. It was weird how the dog reminded him of someone he knew. There was a girl in his class, a really nice girl, who had bright blue eyes and straggly bangs. Her name was Agatha, and she wasn't ugly, just different. She had the best collection of baseball cards in the whole school.

"Listen," Buck said, chuckling. "You wished for a dog, didn't you? Well, here she is."

Corby's heart sank. "That's not funny!" he snapped. "I want a puppy, not—not that one!"

"I was kidding," Buck said, but Corby was getting more worried by the second. Maybe the Wish Master couldn't be bothered with details, like sending the *right* dog. After all, he'd delivered the wrong video game, hadn't he?

The dog started toward them. She walked with an odd kind of shamble, as if her feet were too big and her legs were too long for the skinny rest of her. The strange eyes studied one boy, then the other, before she lay down at Corby's feet.

"She sure acts as if she belongs to you," Buck commented. "Whether you want her or not."

Corby turned and walked fast along the riverbank, toward the path that led back to the road. He had to get home. A puppy might be waiting for him there right now. He tried to think of a way that could happen. Maybe the owners of the Labrador puppies had heard Grandma was sick and had sent a puppy to cheer her up. If so, she'd definitely want Corby to have it.

Buck hurried after him. "Don't look now," he said, "but the dog's right behind you."

"So what?" Corby turned onto the path and started to run. Unexpectedly, the dog shot past him, loping with surprising grace. When she reached the road, she turned and lay down, waiting.

"Listen," Corby told her, "I'm not the person you're looking for. What do you want, anyway?"

The dog stood up, stretched, and plopped hairy front paws on Corby's shoulders. She began to talk—no words but a funny mixture of yips and groans and howls. Corby had never heard anything like it.

"You could let her follow you home," Buck suggested slyly. "I bet your grandpa would know how to scare her off."

Corby winced, imagining what Grandpa would say if he saw this dog. He'd look at that scrawny body and the strange eyes and the scraggly coat, and that was all he'd see. He wouldn't know how friendly she was or how she'd picked Corby for her pal. Or that when she stood on her hind legs and put her paws on your shoulders, she looked as if she were smiling under all that stringy hair. He wouldn't know she could talk.

"My grandpa's not going to see her," Corby said, making up his mind. He patted the dog's chest, feeling the bony ribs under his fingers. "I'll figure out what to do with her. I'm the one who asked for a dog."

CHAPTER SEVEN
Taking Care of a Pal

"Now what?" Buck asked when they reached the road. "If we go any farther, your folks might see her."

"I'm thinking," Corby said.

"You have to have a place for Old Ugly to stay in," Buck said, as if Corby didn't know that. "And you have to feed her and give her some water. I s'pose you could tie her out in the woods—"

"Who lives there?" Corby pointed at one of the summer cottages across the road.

Buck looked alarmed. "That's the Kellers' place—they come up from Milwaukee for a couple of weeks in August. But you can't put her in their house, pea brain! If that's what you want to do, count me out. My dad would kill me!"

Corby glanced at the dog. She was lying down again, with her chin on her paws, waiting.

"I bet the Kellers would let us use their garage if they saw how skinny and tired she is," he said softly.

"No way!" Buck exclaimed. "Listen, you're going to get into a whole lot of trouble, and you don't even know if this is really your dog."

"Well, *she* thinks she's mine," Corby said. "And if I take her home my grandpa might—shoot her!" He hadn't thought of that before, but now it sounded possible.

"No way," Buck repeated, only this time he didn't sound so certain. When Corby and the dog started up the drive to the cottage, he followed them.

The Kellers' garage wasn't locked. A wooden bar resting in rusted brackets held the doors shut. When Corby lifted the bar, the doors swung open.

"See, it's mostly empty," Corby said. "Why would they care if we used it for a while?"

Inside, the air was musty. Late afternoon sun streamed through two small, dirty windows at the back. Empty cartons were heaped in one corner, and there was a stack of burlap bags in the other.

"We can make her a bed in one of those boxes," Corby said. He picked up a burlap bag but dropped it in a hurry when two mice streaked out and ran through the open doors.

"Old Ugly doesn't need a bed," Buck teased. "Look at her."

The dog lay close to Corby's feet. Except for the strange, watchful eyes, she might have been a pile of rags on the dirt floor.

"If you leave her here without food and water, she's going to bark," Buck warned. "Howl, maybe."

Corby frowned. Finding a shelter had been easy, but feeding the dog would be harder. He wondered if he could smuggle leftover stew or some bread crusts without his mother or grandpa noticing.

"Will you stay here with her while I go home and get some stuff?" he asked.

Buck shook his head. "If you're really going to keep her, then *you* stay here, and I'll get some dog food. My dad buys it in forty-pound sacks. Only it'll take awhile because I'll have to eat supper before I come back."

The dog's mismatched eyes were closed now, and she was snoring softly. She was practically telling Corby she trusted him.

"Okay, then," he whispered. "I say we both go home and eat, and we both come back."

"She'll bark for sure if she wakes up," Buck warned again, but he helped Corby close the doors and lift the wooden bar into place.

"It'll be okay," Corby said confidently. "I don't think she'll bark. She'll know I'm coming back."

The barking began while they were eating dessert.

"This is good pie," Grandpa said. "I didn't know California people could make pie this good." He took a final bite and put down his fork. "Listen to that racket! One of the Millers' dogs must have treed a raccoon."

"The poor thing doesn't sound excited," Corby's mother said thoughtfully. "It sounds kind of mournful."

"Mournful because it doesn't know how to climb that tree," Grandpa said. He glanced at Corby. "Reminds me of when your dad and I used to go hunting when he was a boy. Do you hunt with him now?"

"There's no place to hunt where we live," Corby said. He was about to say they did a lot of other things together, but Grandpa grunted impatiently and stood up.

"Your dad used to be a good shot," he said. "He was good at everything he tried." He patted Corby's mother on the shoulder. "I'm going upstairs to see if Meg ate her pie."

Corby waited till he was out of sight. "It's not my fault we don't go hunting," he said angrily. "He hates me."

"Oh, Corby!" His mother shook her head at him. "Stop saying that! Don't even think it. If he sounds cranky, it's because he's unhappy. He'd like everything to be the way it used to be, when he and Grandma were young and healthy." She paused, and they listened to the heavy footsteps in the upstairs hall. "You know, Grandpa walks the way that poor dog sounds. Sad, sad, sad."

Corby didn't feel sorry for Grandpa. After all, Grandma was getting better, wasn't she? And in the meantime he had someone to bake apple pie for him and he had a grandson—the runt of the litter—to pick on. The dog was different. She was alone and maybe just a little bit worried that Corby wasn't going to come back.

"I have to go out for a while," he said, trying to sound offhand. "Buck's coming over."

His mother stared at him. "Now? It'll be dark soon. What are you going to do?"

"Just hang out," Corby said. He edged toward the door. "Is it okay if I take this cottage-cheese container? It's empty."

"I know it's empty." She laughed. "What in the world is going on, Corby? You're up to something."

Corby laughed, too, but at the same time he pushed the screen door and ran down the porch steps, two at a time, before she could ask any more questions. That was the trouble with grown-ups, he thought. They either didn't understand anything, like Grandpa, or they understood too much, like his mother.

CHAPTER EIGHT
Trapped Again!

"Don't call her Old Ugly," Corby said. "Her name is Aggie."

"You're kidding." Buck made a face as he propped his rickety bicycle against a tree. "That's a crazy name for a dog."

"Well, she likes it," Corby retorted. "Before I opened the garage door, I said, 'Aggie, quit barking,' and she did."

"She was just glad somebody was coming to let her out. You could have called her Mudhead. She wouldn't care."

"She likes Aggie," Corby insisted. "You should have seen her jump all over me and try to lick my face."

"Big deal." Buck grinned and pointed at a sack of dog food and a couple of battered tin bowls in the bicycle basket. "You can use one bowl for food and the other for water," he said. "There's probably a pump behind the cottage."

"We already found it," Corby said proudly. "I filled that cottage-cheese container three times before she stopped drinking." He poured some dog food into one of the bowls and watched Aggie dip her nose into it. "I'm going to teach her tricks," he said. "I think she's pretty smart."

"Because she eats when she's hungry?" Buck teased. "How much brains does that take?"

Corby didn't answer. He knew Aggie was smart. He couldn't explain it, but he knew.

"Hey!" Buck said suddenly. "Did you ride horses at that camp you went to?"

Corby nodded. He was trying to decide what tricks he would teach Aggie.

"Well, that's okay then," Buck said. "My dad said you could use one of our horses in the parade, as long as you knew what you were doing. I'm going to be a lawman, and you can be my Indian pal."

"What parade?" Alarmed, Corby jerked his thoughts back to the present. "What are you talking about?"

"The Fourth of July parade," Buck said impatiently. "Berry Hill's parade. Doesn't your grandpa tell you anything? It's really neat. Anybody can be in it who wants to be. It starts and ends at the Campbells' farm—they're on the other side of our place. We go through town, and afterward Mrs. Campbell serves hot dogs and ice cream to everybody in the parade."

Corby bent to scratch Aggie's bony head. "I don't want to," he said in a muffled voice.

"Don't want to what?"

"Be in it," Corby said, not looking up. "I'm going to be pretty busy taking care of my dog."

"You're kidding!" The words practically exploded out of Buck's mouth. "You don't have to be with her every minute, for Pete's sake!"

Corby's face felt hot. "I probably won't even be here on the Fourth of July," he said. "My dad wants me to come home. He's sort of lonesome."

"You're making that up," Buck said angrily. "You don't want to ride because you think the parade sounds corny, just because it won't have big bands and floats and all the city stuff. So who

49

cares what you think!" He grabbed his bike and swung it around toward the road.

"Wait," Corby said unhappily, not sure what to say next. If only he could be sure his second wish were going to come true! "I just meant—I won't have time to learn tricks or anything like that."

"Tricks?" Buck repeated. "Who said anything about tricks? All you have to do is sit on old Josey and ride."

Corby gave up. "Okay," he said. He was trapped again.

Buck eyed him. "Do you swear? Just remember, you wouldn't even have Old Ug—Aggie if I hadn't taken you to the Wish Master."

They both looked at the dog, who peered back at them as if she were eager to see what would happen next.

"I swear," Corby said. "Thanks for bringing the dog food."

When Buck rode away, Corby hoisted the bag of dog food to a rickety shelf and then sat down on the dirt floor of the garage. He'd been on a horse exactly twice at Camp Macaho. Both times he could hardly wait to get off. When he closed his eyes, he had the same sick feeling he'd had then.

"Dogs are lucky," he told Aggie. "You don't know how lucky."

The pale blue eye blinked behind its curtain of gray hair. Then Aggie folded her skinny legs and laid her head on Corby's knee. She seemed to be saying that she did know, and, for a moment at least, the sick feeling faded.

"Good girl," Corby said. "We like each other the way we are, right?"

Aggie sighed and fell asleep.

Aggie never barked again when she was left alone in the garage. Each morning, as Corby neared it, he could hear toenails scratching the door and funny little whimpers of excitement. When he lifted the bar from its braces, the doors burst open so fast he was almost knocked off his feet. Aggie hurtled through the opening and shot around the yard, leaping at tree branches and jumping over stumps. Sometimes she showed off, walking on her hind legs and swatting butterflies. Sometimes she ran in figure eights, snapping at her tail. When she was tired, she skidded to a stop at Corby's feet and rolled over, her skinny legs paddling the air. The pale blue eye looked up as if to say, "Well, how did you like *that?*"

Corby liked it fine.

On the third morning he decided that when Aggie ran she was beautiful. The long bony legs stretched into a graceful lope, and the gray tail curled elegantly over her spine. That afternoon Corby found an old scrubbing brush in Grandpa's shed and brought it with him when he returned to the garage. He brushed Aggie's coat until it shone, noticing that after just three days of Buck's dog food the bony ribs were almost hidden.

Every day they went exploring along little back roads, and Corby tried to teach Aggie to fetch. She always watched with interest as the stick sailed over her head, but she clearly didn't see the point of chasing it. When she did, she was usually gone for several minutes. Once in a while she brought back the stick Corby had thrown, but usually she had found something she liked better. A tiny bluebird's egg. A smelly dead fish. An empty peanut-butter jar. Once she dropped a small gray woodchuck at Corby's feet.

"Bad dog!" Corby scolded, but he couldn't help laughing at the woodchuck's surprised expression. When the little animal waddled back into the brush, Aggie looked as if she were laughing, too.

"It's too bad Buck has to work so much," Corby's mother said when he came home for meals. "What in the world do you find to do all day?"

"I'm fine," Corby said truthfully. The hours he spent with Aggie flew by. It was the evenings that dragged, with Grandpa glaring at him every time he turned on the television set or took out a video game. There was nothing to think about except Buck's parade.

Old Josey. He'd say the name to himself and get goose bumps on his arms. A name didn't tell you a thing. The meanest-tempered horse at Camp Macaho was called Sweetums.

What he needed was a miracle. A telephone call from his dad. Anything! The Wish Master was going to have to get busy, if he and Aggie were to be on their way to California before the Fourth of July.

CHAPTER NINE
A Scrawny Little Nothing

"It's no use checking the weather channel every ten minutes," Corby's mother teased. "The weatherman won't call off a rainstorm for tomorrow just because it happens to be the Fourth of July."

"I know that," Corby said. He glared at the weather map on the screen. There was rain moving toward Berry Hill, but it might go to the north and miss them. Or it might not. He wanted all the clouds in the sky to head right for Berry Hill. He hoped the rain would come down in buckets, with so much lightning and thunder that no one would dare go outside. He had a feeling it would take a super storm to make the town call off its parade.

Grandpa took the remote control out of Corby's hands and switched to the evening news.

"You know how to ride?" he asked, his eyes on the screen.

"We rode at camp." Corby squirmed uneasily.

"That's no answer," Grandpa said, but at that moment the telephone rang and the questions stopped.

"I'll get it!" Corby's mother jumped up. "It'll be your dad, Corby," she said. "We talked for a few minutes this morning, and he said he'd call again tonight. I think he has big news."

Corby shot off the couch as if he were jet-propelled. He reached the kitchen before his mother did, and for the next few minutes he stood on one foot, then the other, listening to her side of the conversation with growing excitement.

"That's wonderful!" his mother said. "When?" Then she said, "He'll be thrilled." And, finally, "You tell him yourself." She handed the phone to Corby, looking so pleased that he decided she must have guessed all along how much he wanted to go home.

"Corby, I wish you were here in Santa Barbara right now."

Corby grinned. Those were the words he'd been hoping to hear.

"I've had a promotion at work—a big one! If you and your mom were here, we'd go out to celebrate. But we'll do it in September for sure."

Corby stared down at the kitchen counter. A new job? *That* was the big news?

"Great," he said weakly.

If he sounded disappointed, his dad didn't seem to notice. "Looks like we'll be able to get the new computer you've been wanting—how about that?"

"Great," Corby said again. "That's really neat, Dad."

"I want to talk to your mom again, and then Grandpa, okay?"

"Okay." Corby handed the phone back to his mother and escaped down the hall.

"Be quiet on those stairs," Grandpa called in a low voice as he passed the den. "If your grandma's awake, tell her I'll be up in a few minutes."

Corby hurried upstairs. Grandma's bedroom door was open a crack, and he peeked in. She was sleeping. He closed the door and tiptoed to his own room, stepping carefully around the creaky spots in the floor.

He pulled off his clothes and climbed into bed. An owl hooted nearby. Any other time, he would have enjoyed the eerie sound, but tonight he hardly noticed it. Tonight there was only one thing to think about. He was stuck here in Berry Hill for the rest of the summer.

He closed his eyes, and the Wish Master popped up behind his eyelids. Go away, Corby thought. Leave me alone. The ugly smiling mouth moved, and even though he clapped his hands over his ears, he knew what the Wish Master was saying:

> *You're a real loser, Corby Hill. You're the kind of kid who thinks he rates two wishes when other people get just one. You hardly listen when your dad tells you something terrific. You're so bad, you even hope it'll rain on the Fourth of July. You're a scrawny little NOTHING!*

Corby groaned, and the owl hooted again. This time it sounded as if it were laughing.

"Glad to meet you, Corby." Mr. Miller shook Corby's hand. "Buck says you're quite a rider. Well, you couldn't have a prettier day to show everybody what you can do."

"Right," Corby mumbled. His Indian costume, a headband with one feather sticking up in back, kept slipping down over his eyebrows.

"Buck's saddling the horses," Mr. Miller went on. "The parade'll come down the road any minute now, and Jim Campbell wants you boys to get in line at the end."

"Right," Corby mumbled again. All morning, as he brushed Aggie's coat and threw sticks for her, he'd practiced saying "No problem" and "Right" in a cheerful voice, but it hadn't helped much.

Hooves clattered inside the barn, and Corby felt his stomach turn over. Buck appeared in the wide doorway leading two horses and wearing a cowboy hat and a cardboard badge covered with tin foil.

"Hey," he yelled, "your feather's crooked." Then he swung up onto the white horse with an ease that made Corby blink.

"I can't do that!" he gasped before he could stop himself.

Mr. Miller chuckled. "Buck's about six inches taller than you, and he's been riding since he was four. He says you learned to ride at camp this summer."

"Right," Corby breathed.

"Well, I'll be glad to give you a lift," Mr. Miller offered cheerfully. "After that, you're on your own." He stood beside the brown horse and cupped his hands below the stirrup. "Her name is Josey. Up you go, boy!"

Corby put one foot into Mr. Miller's hands, and suddenly he was flying. He landed in the saddle with a *thunk*, gripping the reins with one hand and a handful of Josey's mane with the other.

Mr. Miller frowned. "You okay, boy?"

"No problem," Corby squeaked. He forced himself to let go of the mane.

"Here they come!" Buck yelled. "Let's go out to the gate!" His horse reared and Buck waved his hat. Then both horses were moving down the drive in a jolting trot. Corby grabbed Josey's mane again. He wondered if he was going to throw up.

CHAPTER TEN
Disaster

At the edge of the road Buck reined in his horse. Josey stopped behind him.

"There's Uncle Sam," Buck pointed. "That's Jim Campbell, and that's his own beard he's wearing. He grows it every summer for the parade."

Corby stared at the blur of colors moving toward them. Uncle Sam, in red, white, and blue, was driving a pony cart. He waved when he saw the boys. The wave might have been a signal, because a row of drummers just behind him sprang into action. Corby felt Josey tremble at the sudden racket.

The drummers were followed by a man with a bugle and a girl with a trombone that was taller than she was. That was the band. Next, a half dozen little girls pushed decorated doll carriages over the rough gravel. A lady in a blue and white hoopskirt walked behind them, helping the smallest ones to keep up. Boy Scouts and Girl Scouts followed, grinning at Buck and looking curiously at Corby. A clown on a bicycle wobbled in and out of the ruts in the road.

"Here comes my 4-H Club!" Buck yelled above the drums. His horse reared again, and the 4-H marchers cheered. Josey shifted nervously.

Two more clowns, dressed like hoboes and blowing bubbles, marked the end of the parade. Buck gave a whoop and moved out into the road, with Josey right behind him.

Corby hung on. Hanging on was all he'd done at Camp Macaho, he reminded himself, and he'd lived through that. Of course, the camp horses were used to beginners, and they moved along at a steady pace, paying little attention to their riders. Corby saw that Josey played the follow-the-leader game, too. She stayed a few feet behind the white horse and slowed down whenever Buck slowed to give the marchers more room.

At first it wasn't bad at all. The drummers stopped playing, and the parade wound quietly past cornfields and rows of thick green soybean plants. Then Buck yelled and pointed. A small crowd was waiting for them at the first crossroads. The girl with the trombone blew one note—a kind of squawk—and the drummers began again. The clowns walked on their hands and did cartwheels in the dust.

Corby's hands were sweaty as they neared the crowd. All that flag-waving and cheering could scare a horse. He held his breath, but Josey seemed unconcerned.

More people appeared up ahead, some of them sitting on their parked cars. Corby straightened up in the saddle and gave Josey a quick pat. Maybe—*maybe* it was going to be all right. The parade was pretty corny, but no one seemed to care. It was fun, having people cheer and clap as they passed by.

"Hey, Corb!" This time Buck stood up in his stirrups to point. Corby saw his mother standing at Grandpa's gate. Quickly he checked the house to see if Grandma was watching from a bedroom window. If she was, Grandpa would be there with her.

The windows were empty. He relaxed and pushed his headband off his eyebrows. He'd dreaded having Grandpa see him on horseback, but it wasn't going to happen. In another minute they would be past the house.

Then Buck yelled again, just as Corby was about to wave to his mother. Corby's hand froze. A skinny gray shape was streaking down the road.

It couldn't be Aggie! He'd barred the door of the garage that morning. He remembered feeling sorry that the dog would have to be alone all afternoon. Yet there she was, long legs stretched, her tail held high like a plume. And she was aimed like a cannonball at the Berry Hill parade.

What happened next was worse than anything Corby could have imagined. Aggie darted around Uncle Sam's pony cart and leaped from one drummer to the next, telling them noisily how glad she was to see them. Pink and white and yellow doll carriages shot off the road on either side as the little girls scrambled for cover.

"What's she *doing*?" Buck roared. "What's the matter with that dumb dog?"

"She's just—just happy!" Corby yelled back and was sorry at once that he'd answered. Aggie had been trying to kiss the lady in the blue and white hoopskirt, but at the sound of her friend's voice she stopped in mid-jump. Corby scrunched down, trying to hide, but he wasn't fast enough. The clown and his bicycle went in opposite directions as Aggie hurtled past the Scouts and the 4-H Club to reach the horseback riders at the end of the parade.

That was when Josey forgot all about playing follow the leader. She whinnied wildly and kicked at the dog leaping around her. Then she reared. Corby struggled with the reins and shouted at Aggie to go away, but it was no use. He caught a glimpse of his mother's horrified face as the horse bolted through Grandpa's gate with Aggie yelping joyfully behind her.

They raced around the yard, crossing the stone walk and its borders of rosebushes a half dozen times before Corby finally lost his grip and flew out of the saddle. The fall seemed to last forever.

CHAPTER ELEVEN
"She's My Dog."

"Corby, are you all right?" Corby's mother threw her arms around him, while the entire Berry Hill parade watched from the other side of the hedge.

"I'm okay." Corby struggled to free himself. "No problem." But he felt sort of wobbly when he stood up, and he almost fell again when Aggie leaped to lick his face.

"You go away!" Corby's mother hardly ever shouted, but she was shouting now. "What's the matter with you, dog? Look at what you've done!"

Aggie danced out of reach while Corby looked around. Most of the rosebushes were trampled into the ground, the pale petals scattered across the lawn. The front gate hung from one hinge. In a far corner of the yard, Josey stood in a flower bed watching Aggie uneasily.

"Grandpa will kill me," Corby moaned.

"Don't be silly!" his mother said, but she looked toward the house as she said it. Then she turned and smiled at the crowd of wide-eyed marchers. "Thank you all for stopping," she called, "but don't hold up the parade any longer. If someone could please just take that horse . . .?"

Uncle Sam waved at her and motioned the marchers to get back in line. When they had moved away from the gate, Buck stomped into the yard. He didn't look at Corby. Still, Corby knew by the way he walked that he was furious.

"Sorry about the flowers, Mrs. Hill," he said gruffly as he led Josey back to the road.

"It'll be all right," Corby's mother said. "Thank you, Buck. Have a good time."

Uncle Sam waved again, and the parade moved silently down the road. Watching them go, Corby felt worse than ever. It had been a really good parade until he and Aggie had spoiled it.

"Where's Grandpa?" he asked, when the marchers were out of sight.

"He's down in the basement making a little windmill for Grandma's rock garden," his mother said. "She wasn't feeling well enough to get up, and he said he wasn't in the mood for a parade." She looked at the ruined rosebushes and shook her head. "Come inside, Corby. Your elbow is bleeding and your clothes are a mess."

"What'll I do with—her." He motioned toward Aggie who had curled up at Corby's feet.

His mother rolled her eyes. "Take her out to the road and send her on her way," she said sharply. "I just hope she won't follow the parade and cause trouble again."

Corby gulped. "She won't," he said. "She's my dog, Mom. Her name is Aggie."

"You mean—you mean she thinks she belongs to you? That's why she chased your horse?"

Corby nodded. He told his mother how Aggie had found him on the riverbank, and how he and Buck had made a home for her in the Kellers' garage. "She's a really great dog, but she likes to dig," he finished. "She must have dug a hole in the dirt floor to get out."

His mother looked ready to cry. "Oh, Corby," she sighed. "If she's your dog, then you're responsible for her and the damage she's done. Why didn't you tell me about her?" She didn't wait for an answer. "Just bring her along inside then," she said tiredly. "We might as well get this over with. I wish your father was here."

Corby grabbed Aggie's rope collar and followed his mother into the house. When they entered the kitchen, they found Grandpa pouring lemonade into a tall glass.

"What's wrong?" he demanded as soon as he saw their faces. "What's that miserable-looking animal doing here?"

Corby gulped. "She's my dog, Grandpa," he said unsteadily. "I had her locked up, but she got loose and sort of messed up the parade. And she chased my horse and they knocked down the roses in the front yard." He stopped for breath. "I'm really sorry."

Grandpa strode heavily across the kitchen. Corby and his mother and Aggie all shrank back to let him pass. When he reached the front door, he stood looking out through the screen for several seconds.

"It's such a shame—" Corby's mother began, but then Grandpa turned around. His face was red, and his eyes seemed to shoot sparks.

"It'll break your grandma's heart when she sees that," he said in a low voice that was worse than a shout. "If you can't handle a horse you

shouldn't have been on one. And as for that fool
dog"—he glared at Aggie, who was checking the
floor for crumbs—"get her out of this house right
now. I don't ever want to see her again!"

Aggie barked and danced away when Corby
reached for her. She's having a good time,
Corby thought unbelievingly. Chasing Josey was
probably the best fun she ever had. Dumb dog.

It helped, a little, to be mad at someone besides
himself.

CHAPTER TWELVE
"It's My Fault!"

The escape hole was behind the boxes in the corner of the garage. Corby swept dirt and gravel into the opening, packing it firmly, while Aggie watched.

She's probably figuring out how long it'll take to dig her way out again, he thought glumly, but he kept working until there was no sign of the hole. Then he rocked back and sat, cross-legged, on the floor.

"Now what?" He scratched Aggie under the chin. For a few minutes he'd had something to think about besides the parade and the rosebushes and Buck and Grandpa. Now there was nothing to do but remember.

"I s'pose we could run away," he said. "But first we'd have to find another empty garage a long way from Grandpa's house. My mom might give us food and stuff."

Aggie cocked her head and yawned. The pale blue eye shone even though the garage was full of shadows. She looked funny and wise. "Don't be silly," was what she seemed to be saying.

Well, maybe it *was* silly to imagine his mother would let him live in a garage for the rest of the summer. But if he didn't do that, and the Wish Master wasn't going to help him go home to Santa Barbara, what else was there?

Aggie yawned again, as if she were tired of thinking. She stretched out with her head on her paws, and after a moment Corby lay down, too, using her warm, dusty back for a pillow.

"Okay," he sighed, "but sleeping won't change anything. We'll just have to think about it later."

When he woke, Aggie's head was up, her ears perked. In the distance a siren wailed. It was a scary sound that grew louder as they listened. It was coming this way.

71

Corby stumbled to his feet and peeked through the partly opened garage doors. While they slept, clouds had covered the sun, and now a wind swept the grove of trees between the Kellers' place and Grandpa's. Corby felt as if he were still sleeping. The siren and the wind and the heavy gray skies belonged in a bad dream.

"You stay here!" he ordered when Aggie tried to squeeze past him. "There's nothing to see. If the fire was around here, we'd smell smoke."

He sounded more certain than he felt. Aggie pressed against his knees, trembling, as the high-pitched wail turned into a shriek. Something white hurtled past, bouncing over the rough road.

White, not fire-engine red. An ambulance.

Corby squeezed through the narrow opening and slammed the doors behind him. He dropped the wooden bar into place and then he began to run. By the time he reached the road, the siren had stopped. The ambulance was in front of Grandpa's broken gate, and two men in blue uniforms were walking up the stone walk, carrying a stretcher.

Corby stopped next to the hedge and stared. The front door opened before the men reached it. His mother let them inside, then stood in the doorway looking out at the garden.

He wanted to call to her, but his voice wouldn't work. Soon the uniformed men returned, carrying Grandma's tiny form on the stretcher. Grandpa was right behind them. They put the stretcher into the ambulance, and one of the men helped Grandpa inside. The other hurried around to the driver's seat. The ambulance swung into Grandpa's driveway and came back, passing so close to Corby that he could have touched its gleaming side.

"Corby?" His mother had seen him. She came out to the road and waited for him to join her.

"We think Grandma may be having another heart attack," she said softly. "She started having chest pains about a half hour ago."

Terrible thoughts churned through Corby's head. "It'll be my fault if she dies," he whispered.

"Oh, no!" His mother put her arm around his shoulders and hugged him. "Of course it isn't your fault. Grandma doesn't know anything about what happened to the garden. She's been in bed all day."

Corby shivered. He was glad Grandma didn't know about the roses, but that wasn't the worst thing he'd done to her. All of a sudden she was sicker than she'd been since they came to Berry

Hill. She might even die. And if she died, he and his mother wouldn't have to stay there any longer.

The Wish Master was letting him have two wishes at the same time after all.

"Corby, what's the matter with you? Stop looking like that." His mother pulled him gently into the yard. "You ran off without any lunch this noon—how about some pancakes while we wait to hear from Grandpa?"

"I'm not hungry," Corby said. "I just wish—"

"I know. You wish we'd get good news right away," his mother said. "So do I, dear."

Corby finished his wish silently as they walked up the path. I just wish I'd never heard of the Wish Master.

CHAPTER THIRTEEN
Corby Takes a Chance

"Why do I have to go to the Millers'?" Corby hunched in the passenger seat and scowled at the headlight beams tunneling through the dark. "Why can't I stay by myself?"

"Because you can't, that's all," his mother said. "Please don't whine, Corby."

He sank deeper into the seat. Grandpa had called to say he was going to spend the night at the hospital, and his mother had decided she should be there with him. By the time Corby returned from checking on Aggie, it had been all settled. Buck's mother had said she'd be glad to have Corby stay with them overnight.

"Buck won't be glad." Corby tried once more. "He's mad because I spoiled the parade."

"You didn't spoil the parade," his mother said impatiently. "I'm sure they all had a fine time, once they got past our house."

If she was trying to cheer him up, it wasn't working. Corby knew he was going to be awake all night, wherever he stayed. The parade was only a part of what wouldn't let him sleep—the smallest part. What was much worse was the terrible thing he had done to Grandma with his second wish. If she died, he wanted to die, too.

When they pulled up in front of the Millers' farmhouse, Buck's mother was waiting on the porch. Two big dogs rushed to meet them.

"Buck went off to bed an hour ago," Mrs. Miller told them. "So did his dad. They just plain wore themselves out at the Campbells' this evening. Seems as if everyone for miles around came for the food and the fireworks. I'm sorry you missed it, Corby." She patted his shoulder and then started talking to his mother about Grandma. Corby sat on a step and waited.

"Do you want a glass of milk and some cookies before you go up to bed?" Mrs. Miller asked when his mother had driven away. "Buck usually has to have a snack at bedtime, only not tonight. I hate to think how many hamburgers that boy must have eaten."

Corby said he wasn't hungry, and together they went upstairs. "The bathroom's here, and that's Buck's room back there." Mrs. Miller pointed. "There's twin beds, so you just make yourself comfortable, Corby. And don't worry about waking Buck. He's a sound sleeper."

When she'd said good night and gone back downstairs, Corby went to the door of Buck's room and looked in. There was a faint sound of snoring from the bed near the open window.

He took off his sneakers and lay down on the other bed. It would help if he could talk, but he didn't want anyone to know what he had done. The thought was like a heavy weight pressing on his chest.

If he could take back that wish, he would gladly stay at Berry Hill all summer. He wouldn't care what Grandpa said or did. If there were some way to take it back. . . .

He sat up. "Hey, Buck."

The shape in the other bed didn't move.

"Hey, are you awake?" His voice was a little louder this time. Buck snorted and sighed. Then he rolled over, and Corby saw his eyes open wide.

"It's me, Corby. My folks are at the hospital with my grandma. I'm sorry about the parade. Aggie—"

"Don't blame Aggie," Buck said sourly. His voice was thick with sleep. "You lied! You said you could ride, but you couldn't even handle old Josey. You told me you learned to ride at camp."

"I didn't say that exactly," Corby protested, but he supposed Buck was right. Maybe he hadn't said the words, but he'd let Buck think them.

"Anyway, I'm sorry," he said again.

"So why did you wake me up?"

Corby took a deep breath. "I was wondering if you want to go to the Wish Master again tonight," he said. "As long as I'm sleeping over and all."

"No way!" Buck grunted disgustedly. "Pipe down, will you? You'll wake up my dad, and he's mad at you, too."

Corby lay back and stared into the dark. If Buck wouldn't go, he might as well forget about asking the Wish Master to take back his wish. Finding the way to the top of the cliff alone would be impossible. It would be a whole lot scarier than the plank bridge at Camp Macaho or the rock wall behind the mess hall. He couldn't do it.

Could he?

A clock chimed eleven downstairs. Corby heard Mrs. Miller tell the dogs it was time for bed. He listened to the slap of her slippers and the clicking of the dogs' toenails on the stairs and in the front bedroom. The dogs flopped down, sighing. A moment later the bedroom door closed softly.

Corby dangled his feet over the side of the bed and reached for the clock on the table between the beds. He'd have to feel his way down the hall and the curving flight of stairs. Mrs. Miller had probably locked the doors, but maybe she hung the key from a hinge, the way Grandpa did. He stood up.

One step into the hall told him he'd never get downstairs without being caught. The floor squeaked, even worse than the floor at Grandpa's house. He hadn't noticed it when the lights were on and Mrs. Miller was beside him, but now the squeak seemed as loud as a siren. One of the dogs in the front bedroom grumbled sleepily.

How did Buck get past the squeaks and the dogs when he wanted to visit the Wish Master? Corby stepped back into the bedroom. There was another way, of course. He just hadn't wanted to think about it. When Buck sneaked out, he left through the window. Corby tiptoed across the room and looked out. There was a shed just below, with a long sloping roof that began about three feet below the windowsill. Buck would slide down the roof—on his seat? On his stomach? There was nothing to hang on to, nothing to do but jump when you reached the edge, but Buck wouldn't care about that. He'd call it fun.

Buck would have been the first kid at Camp Macaho to run across the plank bridge.

CHAPTER FOURTEEN
Finding the Wish Master

It wasn't fun, but it was fast. Corby skidded down the roof on his seat, starting slowly and gaining speed as he went. Near the bottom, he flopped backward and pressed his heels hard against the shingles.

A cloud with silvery edges covered the moon. He waited, his heart thudding, until the cloud drifted off. Then he shifted Buck's little clock from his front pocket to a back one, turned over, and dangled his legs in space. To his surprise, his toes brushed something hard. He slid down an inch, then another, until he stood on a bumpy surface.

It was a woodpile. He turned around, and the chunks of wood moved under his feet. There was nothing to do but jump. He landed hard but didn't fall. As he raced around the side of the house he heard logs tumbling over each other.

Could the Millers sleep through that much noise? He reached the road and glanced over his shoulder, expecting to see lights upstairs. Maybe Mr. Miller had a gun next to his bed to scare off prowlers. That thought made him run even faster, until he could no longer make out the dark hulk of the farmhouse. Then he slowed to a walk, straining to see what lay ahead as another cloud hid the moon.

Nothing to be afraid of around here, he reminded himself. Just corn and beans. But his footsteps seemed louder than they did in the daylight. And he hadn't noticed before that wind blowing through cornstalks sounded like whispers.

He hurried along the road, running when there was enough light, slowing down when clouds closed in. There was a rain smell in the air. Just this morning he'd been hoping rain would stop the parade, but he didn't want it now. Finding the way to the Wish Master was going to be hard enough without a storm to make it worse.

He had stopped to tie a sneaker when he heard someone, or something, running toward him.

Seconds later Aggie leaped against his chest and covered his face with sloppy kisses.

"What are you doing here?" he demanded, his voice shaky with relief. "You're supposed to be asleep in the garage!"

Aggie planted her forepaws on his shoulders and talked. It made Corby feel about ten thousand times better, just listening to her.

He walked faster. Fields gave way to lawns and gardens, and then they reached Grandpa's house. Corby shivered. A few hours ago he'd stood here, at the end of the hedge, watching as Grandma was carried to the ambulance. *My fault!* he thought again. It's all my fault. He touched Aggie's shaggy head and walked on, past the Kellers' place and the two cottages beyond it. Now the road was lined with meadows.

"Keep watching for the start of the path," he told Aggie. "On *this* side of the road, dopey!"

Aggie was having a great time, dashing from one side of the road to the other, with her nose close to the ground. She acted as if—as if she explored this road every night. Maybe she does, he thought. Maybe she's been coming and going through the hole in the corner of the garage whenever she feels like it.

Twice he thought he saw the start of the path through the tall meadow grass, but each time he turned back. When he hesitated a third time, Aggie kept going. She plunged deep into the meadow and disappeared from sight, except for her tail.

Desperate, Corby followed the tail. The direction felt right, but he couldn't be sure. He hoped Aggie's smart nose had found the path he and Buck had used on their visits to the Wish Master.

Thunder growled in the distance like an angry bear. "Gotta hurry!" he mumbled, and Aggie bounded to his side. She danced on her hind legs, talking her weird Aggie talk, and then she tried to return the way they had come.

"No!" Corby grabbed her rope collar and held on. "Find the woods," he ordered. "Let's go!"

A few more steps showed him that Aggie had already found the woods. That was why she had turned back. Pine needles scraped his forehead, and he realized that the darker than dark in front of him was the wall of trees.

Aggie liked open fields. She let Corby drag her along until he found Buck's marker, but she yelped when he swept aside the nearest branch and pulled her through the opening.

"It's okay," he told her. "We can still see the path. Sort of. I know there's a log we have to get over, and then there's a low place, and after that we start climbing. We'll be at the top of the cliff before you know it."

Aggie groaned. "It's okay," Corby said again. "Nothing to worry about."

He moved slowly, one arm outstretched to push aside low branches, and the fingers of the other hand hooked firmly through Aggie's collar. "Nothing to it, see? Just keep moving—"

There was a rustling sound off to the left. "That's a rabbit," Corby whispered hoarsely. "I can tell. Or it might be a raccoon. He won't bother us if we don't bother him."

Aggie quivered and pressed against his knee. She was letting him know she didn't believe a word of it.

"Listen," Corby said, "pretend we're hiking down the road and the sun is shining and you're chasing butterflies and"—thunder rumbled again, much closer this time—"and anyway, we're nearly there. See how steep it's getting. Pretty soon we'll hear the river, and that'll mean we're almost to the top of the cliff."

He stopped to catch his breath and study the face of Buck's little clock. It was too dark to read the numbers, but the glowing hands told him the time. Ten minutes before twelve.

Ten minutes! Were they really close to the top of the cliff? He climbed faster, stumbling over roots, with Aggie whimpering and tugging him backward. The moon was hidden completely by clouds.

"There! Can you hear the water?" Corby pictured the river rushing along below them. He tightened his grip on Aggie's collar and with his right hand clutched at branches, underbrush, *anything* to keep from slipping toward the cliff's edge. Raindrops splattered his face.

"Just a little bit farther," he panted. He stumbled again, and when he scrambled to his feet he was standing on the rocky platform he remembered.

"Good girl!" His knees were shaking, but that didn't matter. He'd made it. Aggie pressed close and sat on his foot.

A flash of lightning gave Corby a glimpse of the Wish Master. He looked even bigger and uglier than the last time. *Greedy kid* was what the Wish Master had called him in his dream. *You're a scrawny little nothing!*

Corby took out the clock and waited for another lightning bolt. It was two minutes to twelve. He started to count, "One-one thousand, two-one thousand, three-one thousand. . . ."

He was soaked, and so was Aggie. It had probably been dumb to think the Wish Master would grant him another wish, no matter how important it was. But he kept counting, anyway. He had reached forty-five seconds of the second minute when the lightning flashed again, followed by a roar of thunder. This time Aggie saw the Wish Master, too. She gave a terrified yelp and leaped backward, pulling Corby off his feet.

"Sixty!" He struggled to get up and shouted his wish into the wind:

"I'M SORRY I TOLD YOU I WANTED TO GO HOME. I DON'T! I JUST WISH MY GRANDMA WOULD GET BETTER. PLEASE!"

The world seemed to fly apart as he said it. Lightning crisscrossed the sky and thunder crashed right overhead.

"Why didn't you wish for that in the first place, pea brain?" a voice jeered from the darkness.

CHAPTER FIFTEEN
"She's Going to Fall!"

"Get away from there, dopey," the voice yelled. "You want to be hit by lightning?"

Speechless, Corby followed the beam of a flashlight to where it began at the top of the path.

"I knew you were up here," Buck said accusingly. "Soon as I saw the bed was empty and my clock was gone. How come you didn't steal my flashlight, too?"

"I didn't know where it was," Corby admitted. "Why did you follow me? I was going to come back before anyone woke up."

"Oh, sure," Buck said sarcastically. His cowboy hat sagged in the rain. "How'd you think you were going to get back in?"

Corby shrugged. He hadn't planned that far ahead.

"There's a ladder behind the toolshed," Buck said. "What you do is, you jump down from the edge of the roof—it isn't that high—and you use the ladder to get back in. Then you have to be the first person outside in the morning so you can put the ladder away. You made a real mess of our woodpile, did you know that?"

He started down the path without waiting for an answer, and Corby followed.

"Well, anyway, we got here," Corby said. "And we didn't need a flashlight either!"

The light swung around. "What do you mean, *we?*" Buck demanded. "You and who else?"

"Me and—" Corby stopped. "Me and my dog!" he said, feeling around frantically in the dark for rough, wet fur. "Where'd she go?"

"How should I know?" Buck asked disgustedly. "That dumb dog could be anywhere."

"She's not dumb," Corby said. When had Aggie disappeared? He remembered the moment just before midnight when she had pulled so hard that he'd lost his balance. That must have been when she took off. He'd been thinking about making his wish and hadn't noticed her go.

89

"Well, I have to find her," he said. "She didn't want to come up here—I made her do it. It's my fault if she's lost."

"Dogs don't get lost," Buck retorted. "She'll sniff around till she finds the path, and then she'll go down the same way you came up."

Corby wasn't sure. "She's afraid of the woods. What if she runs into a bear? What if she can't find the path in the rain?"

"Listen," Buck said, "we have to go back right now. I sneaked out a couple of times last summer, and my dad said if I did it again I'd be in big trouble. If he finds out, he probably won't even let me order my bike—and that'll be your fault, too! You keep making wishes, and I haven't gotten my first one!"

Corby called "Aggie!" a couple of times and strained to hear an answering bark. Then, unhappily, he followed the bobbing flashlight down the path. Aggie had a way of appearing where he didn't expect her, he reminded himself. Maybe this would be one of those times.

Going downhill turned out to be even harder than going up. The path was muddy and littered with wet leaves. Once, Buck dropped the flashlight when he fell, and they watched helplessly as it rolled ahead of them. When it stopped against the root of a tree, Buck crawled on hands and knees to get it.

"Good thing it didn't go the other way," he muttered. "We're really close to the river here."

Corby clung to a bush and listened to the faint rush of the river. Then he heard something else, half whimper, half yelp.

Aggie-talk.

"She's here!" he shouted. "Hey, Buck, I can hear her!"

The yelping grew louder. Corby felt sick as he realized where the sound came from. He dropped to his knees and crawled off the path toward the edge of the cliff.

Buck wiped the muddy flashlight on his shirt and came after him. "Go slow," he warned. "The water's real rough here—lots of rocks. I know you can swim but—"

"She's not in the water," Corby panted. "She's stuck somewhere. Hey, Aggie!"

He reached ahead for something to hold on to and found empty space instead. The rain-soaked earth was slick under his knees, and he scooped up handfuls of mud as he tried to stop his slide. Then he felt Buck's hand close around one ankle.

A moment later the flashlight beam settled on a thick root sticking out from the bank. He grabbed it with his right hand and waited, gasping for breath, till Buck crawled up beside him. Flat on their stomachs, they peered over the rim of the cliff.

Aggie was just below them on a ledge not much wider than she was. When she saw Corby, she wriggled with joy and almost slipped off into the water below.

Corby pulled back. "You talk to her," he whispered, "and keep the light off me. I'll try to grab her collar."

"What's the use?" Buck demanded. "We can't pull her up that way—she's too heavy. She'll choke!"

"Just do it!" Corby said fiercely. "If I don't hold on to her, she's going to fall for sure."

Buck groaned but did as he was told. "Okay, goofy dog," he said in a suddenly gentle voice Corby had never heard him use before. "You're too goofy to stay on the path . . . what a dog. . . I never saw such a goofy dog. . . ."

Corby tightened his grip on the root and stretched. The fingers of his left hand grazed Aggie's bony head and slid under the rope collar.

"Got her!" He was weak with relief. "It's okay, Aggie, don't move!"

"It's not okay," Buck argued, back to his normal voice. "Now what?"

Corby thought fast, trying to come up with a plan. "As long as I hold her, she can't fall," he said. *Unless the collar slips. Unless my arm breaks off!* "You better go home and get some rope. Or leather straps—that would be better! We need something to haul her up with."

"How am I supposed to do that!" Buck growled. "That kind of stuff is all in the barn, and I could never get the door open without my dad hearing. It creaks something awful—he says it's better than a burglar alarm."

Corby's shoulders ached. His nose itched, but with one hand clutching Aggie's collar and the other clamped around the root, he couldn't scratch.

"Well, if he does wake up—" he hesitated, "I don't think he'd be so mad if you told him about Aggie—"

"NO!" Buck scrambled back from the edge of the cliff, taking the light with him. "I told you, I'm not telling him anything! Listen," he went on, "we both should go back right now. Aggie will be okay.

Tomorrow morning we can get all the stuff we need to pull her up."

Corby was silent.

"I'm going then," Buck threatened. "And I feel sorry for you if a bear comes along!"

When Corby still didn't reply, Buck exploded. "I'm never going to get my bike!" he yelled. "The only thing I'm going to get is a beating if my dad finds out why you came up here. He'll blame me if you drown or break your neck!"

Corby shuddered. "I won't," he said, and pressed his knuckles into Aggie's fur. She was trembling terribly. "If she was your dog, I bet you'd stay."

It took awhile before he realized the argument was over. Buck was no longer there.

The rain let up for a while and then came down harder than ever, pressing Corby into the mud with needle-sharp fingers. Corby hoped Aggie couldn't tell how scared he was. His shoulders throbbed, and he couldn't feel his hands at all. If a bear did come along . . .

"There aren't any bears. Buck made that up." He was pretty sure of it, but saying the words helped. "All we have to do is hold on, Aggie."

He tried to figure out how far Buck might have gone by now. The Millers' farm was a long way off—halfway around the world! And when Buck got there he'd have to sneak into the barn to find what they needed, and then he'd have to come all the way back. It would take a very long time.

Aggie whimpered as if she knew what he was thinking. Then, to Corby's horror, she tried to lie down. The collar bit into her neck, and she lurched sideways.

"No, Aggie!" He slid forward, scraping his chin on something sharp. Desperately, he clung to the collar and pulled. At last, just as the pain in his shoulders was becoming unbearable, she regained her balance and stopped struggling.

"Good girl!" Corby hung over the edge. He was afraid to move or even take a deep breath. His head felt as if it were full of rocks, pulling him down, and he wondered if this was what fainting felt like. If he fainted, he and Aggie would both fall. The river would carry them away—he could see it happening, like a movie or a dream. Tomorrow someone would find them, still together, and feel very sad. "What a brave kid!" the person would say. "He gave his life for his dog!"

Then the dream vanished, and the churning water leaped up at him in a blaze of light. A hard hand gripped his shoulder.

"If there's any more ways to get into trouble," a deep voice rumbled, "I guess you'll find 'em!"

Corby managed to turn his head. Grandpa Hill was crouched in the mud, looking down at Aggie. Behind him, Buck held a lantern, his face spooky white in its glare.

CHAPTER SIXTEEN
"A Kind
of Snowman"

He was sitting in the kitchen drinking cocoa, but Corby couldn't remember how he got there. What he did remember was Grandpa leaning over the edge of the cliff and lifting Aggie as if she weighed about as much as a feather. The next minute, it seemed, they were home, and his mother was hugging and scolding and handing out dry clothes, all at the same time.

"Is Grandma really okay?" Corby could hardly believe it. The Wish Master had worked very fast.

"She's sound asleep," his mother said happily. She hugged him again. "It wasn't a heart attack after all, thank goodness. Her doctor said we might as well come home—and it's a good thing we did! What if we hadn't been here when Buck came to the door?"

"I would have kept on going," Buck said. "I only stopped because I saw the lights. My folks don't know I—we—I mean, they think we're still in bed."

"You mean you sneaked out?" Grandpa growled. "Call it what it is."

"But *why*?" Corby's mother waited for an answer, but the boys just looked at each other. "Corby, Buck told us you went up on that cliff to make a wish. He said you were worried about Grandma, so you went out in the middle of the night in a storm. Does that make sense?"

Strange sounds came from under the table. Aggie was talking in her sleep.

Corby's mother tried not to smile. "That doesn't answer my question," she said. But then, to Corby's relief, she changed the subject. "I'm going to drive you home, Buck. There's been enough wandering around in the rain for one night."

"You can't!" Buck exclaimed in a panicky voice. "I don't want my folks to know I—we—sneaked out."

"But they're going to find out sooner or later," Corby's mother protested. "In the morning, when they see Corby is gone, you'll have to tell them what happened. If you don't, they'll call here and I'll tell them. You did a very brave thing, going to find Corby and then running for help. Your parents will be proud of you."

Buck looked doubtful, but he waited at the door while she got her raincoat and Grandpa's car keys.

"Corby, you finish your cocoa and go to bed," she ordered. "And don't worry about Buck. I'll see to it that his parents understand."

As soon as they were gone, Corby stood up. Scrambling sounds came from under the table as Aggie struggled to stand up, too. She looked weirder than ever—mud-streaked and skinny, with hair hanging like a curtain over her eyes.

"So you went out and nearly got yourself killed so you could wish your grandma would get better." Grandpa shook his head. "Your ma was right—it was a dumb thing to do. Your grandma might not think so, but I do."

"It wasn't so dumb." Corby said. "She *is* better, isn't she?" He tried to explain. "There's a big stone *thing* up there that makes your wishes come true. It's called the Wish Master. I wished for a video game and I got one, and I wished for a dog and I got Aggie. Buck wished for a mountain bike, and his dad says he can order one as soon as he finishes cleaning the barn. Maybe the Wish Master doesn't always get things straight, but he tries. Like with Grandma."

"If that dog is the best he could send you, you should have given up," Grandpa said. "What do you mean, 'like with Grandma'?"

Corby met Grandpa's fierce glare. He hadn't meant to tell anyone—especially Grandpa—what he had done. Now he was trapped.

"It was my fault she had to go to the hospital," he said softly. "I told the Wish Master I wanted to go home right away, and I guess he thought if Grandma died . . ."

"If Grandma died, you and your ma could pack up and head back to California." Grandpa finished the sentence for him. They stared at each other.

"What's your big hurry?" Grandpa asked after a minute. "What's wrong with a summer in Berry Hill? Best place in the world, I'd say."

Corby took a deep breath. "You don't like runts," he said. "I heard you say it—runt of the litter. I'm just in the way around here. But I never meant for Grandma to die so I could go home.

That's why I went back tonight. I wanted to make the Wish Master understand."

By the time he finished his explanation, Grandpa's face had turned a dark red.

"I never said you were in the way," he grumbled. Then he pointed at Corby's chair. "Sit down a minute and I'll tell you a story that'll save you a trip in the dark the next time you think of something you want."

Corby sat.

"This happened when I was in high school. It was homecoming weekend and we were all on the football team. We were pretty worked up, waiting for the big game that evening." He paused. "Are you on any teams at school?"

"No," Corby said.

"Well, if you were you'd know how we felt. Uptight, wanting to get started. We hung around town for a while, and then we decided to take a hike. The whole team went—our girlfriends, too. Grandma was with me. She was a cheerleader."

Corby blinked. It wasn't hard to imagine Grandpa playing football, but he couldn't picture Grandma in a cheerleader's outfit.

"We walked up to the highest point overlooking the river—that's where you were tonight.

When we got there, somebody noticed a tall hunk of rock standing by itself. There were other rocks scattered around, and we decided to build a kind of snowman."

"A snowman?" Corby repeated.

"A snowman, made of *rocks*," Grandpa said impatiently. "It was just something to do until game time. Hard work, too! One of the boys had a marking pen in his shirt pocket. He drew a face on another big boulder, and we hoisted it up on top of the first one. When we finished, we took turns writing our initials, upside down and backward, all over the thing. And then we hiked back to town to get ready for the game. I never thought about it again till tonight when Buck came banging on the door. On the way to the cliff he told me why you'd gone up there."

"*You* made the Wish Master?" Corby could hardly believe it. "Does Buck know?"

"I didn't feel like talking then," Grandpa said. "Not while I was wondering whether we'd find you on the cliff or at the bottom of the river."

Corby thought about the strange events of the last couple of weeks. "Are you sure that's all it is?" he asked doubtfully. "A pile of rocks?"

"A Kind of Snowman"

"Far as I know. Somebody must have made up the rest a long time ago, and folks have been believing it ever since. Some people believe whatever you tell 'em."

Dumb people like me, Corby thought. He pushed back his chair. "I'm going to bed," he mumbled, and hurried down the hall with Aggie close behind him.

He wouldn't feel so bad, he thought, if Grandpa hadn't been the one who'd told him the truth. It was a relief to know the Wish Master hadn't made Grandma sick. He hadn't sent Aggie either. Aggie had been looking for a friend, and she'd chosen Corby.

He climbed into bed and Aggie jumped up beside him. She was already snoring when Grandpa trudged up the stairs a few minutes later.

"You asleep?"

Corby lay very still with his eyes closed.

"If you are, that's okay. I was just going to say, you sure made me think of your pa tonight. What you did was the same kind of stunt he might have pulled at your age. Once he made up his mind to do something, you couldn't stop him. Didn't matter how scared he was."

Corby's eyes flew open, and Grandpa snorted. "I thought so," he said. "We'll talk tomorrow about where that sorry-looking dog is going to sleep."

He closed the door and left Corby to stare into the darkness. It was the first time anyone had ever, *ever* said he was like his dad. He repeated the words out loud: "You couldn't stop him. Didn't matter how scared he was."

That's me, he whispered to Aggie, and she yawned, as if she'd known it all the time.